G000091406

*By Matthew Kneale*

Mr Foreigner

Inside Rose's Kingdom

Sweet Thames

English Passengers

Small Crimes in an Age of Abundance

# Matthew Kneale

# Powder

PICADOR SHOTS

First published 2006 by Picador
an imprint of Pan Macmillan Ltd
Pan Macmillan, 20 New Wharf Road, London N1 9RR
Basingstoke and Oxford
Associated companies throughout the world
www.panmacmillan.com

ISBN-13: 978-0-330-44575-7
ISBN-10: 0-330-44575-8



1 3 5 7 9 8 6 4 2

A CIP catalogue record for this book is available from
the British Library.

Typeset by Intype Libra Ltd
Printed and bound in Great Britain by
Mackays of Chatham plc, Chatham, Kent

PETER PELHAM WAS AWARE that something odd was happening as he walked Romulus across the common that bright spring evening. First there was the stranger, who was wearing quite the wrong clothes for exercise, who ran suddenly past him, barging his arm. Next, as if in answer to the question just forming in Peter's mind, there was the slow wail of a police siren. Peter Pelham was no vigilante, anything but. It never entered his thoughts to give chase, or even to complain at being barged, and he merely frowned silently to himself, tugging at Romulus's leash to stop him barking. Only when the fugitive – or whatever he was – had safely disappeared behind a blackberry bush did Peter mutter, with sudden venom, 'Stupid prat.' It was all over in a moment, just another small incident of London life, best left well alone, and it was already fading from Peter's mind when he stopped at a bench to sit and wait while Romulus struggled to defecate. Peter was staring at Romulus's greying muzzle and thinking vaguely of vets' bills when he heard a beeping sound from beneath the slats of the bench. It was, unmistakably, the ring of a cellphone, playing 'Speed Bonny Boat'. Peter let it ring once, twice, three times. On another evening he might have ignored it but today for some reason he was curious. Glancing down he saw a black holdall and, reaching inside, his hand found the cellphone, resting on top of what felt like groceries.

'Hello?'

'Larry? Is that you?'

'Actually, no.' Peter wondered how to explain this strange situation. Already his professionally trained mind was scanning for illegalities but as far as he could see there was nothing against the law about answering an abandoned phone. 'You see . . .'

The line went dead.

It was only then that Peter pulled out the holdall and saw it was filled with small plastic bags, each clear and filled with fine white powder like flour. He dropped the cellphone back in shock. Now finally he made the connection, remembering that the man who had barged him had been carrying one just the same. For a moment he was tempted just to shove it back beneath the bench and go, but he knew he could not. A lawyer might not be expected to play vigilante but he should try to uphold the law, and so Peter got to his feet, picked up the bag, tugged at Romulus's leash and set out for the police station. The bag was surprisingly heavy and he shifted it from shoulder to shoulder, hand to hand. As he went he found himself troubled by the thought – which he knew was absurd – that he might be stopped by the police, and they would jump to all the wrong conclusions. His mind was still playing with headlines – 'Solicitor arrested in drugs haul' – when he was surprised by the sight of his own blue-painted front door. He had not gone to the police station after all but, from habit, had walked home. He turned around, ignoring Romulus's puzzled whine, and stepped back into the street. So far he had done nothing remotely reprehensible, and it was only now that his behaviour became strange. First he stopped on the pavement, standing motionless like a mannequin as he stared with great concentration in the direction of a No Dumping sign. A plane flew overhead, catching him for an instant in the blink of its shadow. Next he glanced up and down the residential street, almost like a criminal, to see if anyone was watching. Nobody was. And then Peter Pelham, dependable London solicitor, who had never broken the law in his life beyond the occasional parking ticket, walked round to the side of his house, unlocked the garage door and, breathing fast, swung it open and marched inside with his black holdall of drugs.

Long afterwards he would consider that this action was an aberration of character, entering a plea – to himself – of temporary insanity. But was this really true? For a long time there had been a discontent about Peter Pelham: the anger of one who feels that life has treated him unfairly. What made this surprising was that almost anybody would have agreed that he was rather fortunate. Everything about him said so. He was a solicitor with a well-established firm, his wife Harriet worked part time for a charity run by a baronet's sister and they lived in one of London's more exclusive suburbs: a leafy ex-village with a pond, an old church and a growing number of celebrity residents. And yet Peter did not think of himself as fortunate at all. He was constantly worrying about money. It seemed simply to pass through him like over-spiced food, and hardly a day went by without some new sum being nibbled away. There were mortgage payments, pension payments, the children's school and university fees, household bills, private health bills, insurance bills, credit card bills. To say nothing of Car Tax, Council Tax and, of course, Income Tax. All in all it was a rare day when the Pelham current account was not overdrawn and accruing bank charges.

The root cause of his troubles, as Peter was only too aware, was his career. It was not that this had gone wrong so much as that it had stopped going right. Once – so long ago that now it seemed hard to believe it had ever been the case – he had been a promising new recruit to McLeans, a leading firm of solicitors, and he had gone to work each morning full of hungry confidence. But then something unconscionable happened: nothing happened. He waited patiently for the moment when he would be told the good news that he had been chosen as an equity partner, but somehow it never came. Several years slipped by and he was still a lowly salaried partner, a temporary state of being, not really a partner at all. His panic grew as he saw others in the firm – others newer and younger than himself – slip past him, like so many queue jumpers. He could not understand it and would lie awake in the night angrily wondering why. Had he made some mistake? There had been a few it was true, but nothing, surely, to warrant this? Had he offended someone? Did he have an enemy? Another possibility – that he was seen as a poor addition to the firm, unable to contribute to the general wealth – was too painful to consider.

'You haven't had much luck bringing in clients, have you?' remarked a colleague one day over lunch: a lunch that Peter guessed afterwards had been set into motion by others. 'That makes things very awkward.'

Peter took the hint and reluctantly began looking round for somewhere less exalted to step down to. Blakeys seemed just the place. It was not such a bad firm and they assured him he would make full partner soon enough. And then, unbelievably, it all happened again: time slipped by and nothing happened. Peter veered between finding reasons – the economic downturn, the firm's troubles – and simple anger. How dare they? They had promised. They were liars and cheats. At night he sometimes dreamed of revenge – a gory massacre of equity partners – but in the morning he went meekly to the office just as usual. Should he try again, lowering his sights further, and look for something outside London, or even in another area of the law? The thought occurred to him, often, but somehow it never took root. He had no wish to do either. Staring at his face in the mirror in the morning as he shaved he could see something had changed, as if some spark had faded from his eyes, and he had adapted to match his failure. Nobody sacked him and so he remained at Blakeys, not by decision but from inertia, aware of the changing glances of others as his position in the firm became increasingly eccentric: a salaried partner who had become somehow stuck, like a caterpillar barred from the cocoon.

If this were not provocation enough, there was also the dreadful business of the Pelhams' neighbours. When Peter and his family had first come to live on Wilmshurst Avenue it had been far from fashionable, possessing a kind of flea-bitten gentility, with cars shrouded beneath plastic mackintoshes. The Pelhams' neighbours had included a taxi driver, a madwoman with moss growing under her car and someone who worked for the BBC. Peter and Harriet enjoyed thinking of themselves as a flagship of grandeur. Since then, though, the area had changed beyond all recognition. Skips came and went as young arrivals set their money to work, violently improving their new properties. Now the High Street gleamed with *croissanteries*, the car mackintoshes and the mad woman's moss had long been displaced by Range Rovers, and it was the Pelhams who felt flea-bitten. Not that anyone was unkind to them – people always smiled and said hello on the street – and yet they felt themselves somehow looked down upon: they were rarely invited to the fashionable parties that they glimpsed through front windows, with marquees squashed into back gardens. At times Harriet grew quite angry.

'No wonder people think we're odd,' she complained one evening as they loaded the dish-washer. 'We must be the only people on the street who haven't built an extension.'

For Peter there were more pressing concerns. He had accidentally scraped his car against a wall, denting the metalwork and, fearing the shame of a bounced cheque, had put off having it repaired. Now two months had passed, the scrape still glowered at him reproachfully and he had begun to make light-hearted remarks to neighbours. 'Isn't it awful. I'm surprised we haven't been run out of the neighbourhood for lowering the tone. Actually we've been meaning to get it done for ages, but we've both been so busy . . .' Money, money, everything was money,

Peter would reflect, during moments, which struck him from time to time, of disgust at the materialistic world in which he lived. There were also moments of sudden panic. From his childhood days Peter had always assumed that he was destined to be in some way remarkable. Now he was in his fifties, stumbling slowly towards the horror of his vanishing point, and this showed no sign of happening. He was utterly replaceable. How had this come to pass? It simply was not right.

And then, that bright spring evening, he found the black holdall beneath the slats of the bench. His only experience of drugs till then was a joint at a university party, which had made him violently sick. He was not even certain what substance this was. And yet, as he stood on the pavement in front of his house, listening to the drone of aircraft engines overhead, he knew precisely what he was holding in his hand. He was holding concentrated danger that, in one brief instant, could destroy every one of his fifty-three years of cautious, law-abiding life. He was holding something of vast, unknown value. Most of all he was holding a piece of chance, dropped from heaven. Peter had never thought of himself as lucky – he was the sort of person who never won lottery money or found a banknote on the ground – and if anything overcame his sense of fear that evening and lured him to the garage door it was the feeling that this windfall was something he was owed. As to what he might do with it, he had little clear idea. Not yet. What had carried him forward, more than anything, was an angry urge to hoard.

Already, with his criminality only a few seconds old and still easily reversible, there were worries. Harriet would be home soon. He knew this was something he could not explain to her. There was an old-fashioned Puritanism to his wife that displayed itself most clearly as she sat over the Sunday papers, when she would comment with clipped approval on new prison sentences, especially those handed down to fallen professionals, from molester priests to embezzling college bursars. It was the pleasure of finding others far worse off than themselves. Peter knew she would never understand about the bag full of bags, which, for that matter, he barely understood himself. And yet he did not like the thought of keeping her in the dark. Their marriage had long ceased to contain the passion of the romantic films that she liked to watch, and yet in a curious way it was not such a bad marriage, based as it was on a kind of camaraderie of family management, and until now any falsehoods between them had been small ones. For a moment Peter hesitated, wondering if he should walk out of the garage and go to the police station after all. It was his anger that held him back. This was his redress. How dare anyone take it from him?

Oddly enough, in view of Peter's profession, the one thing that did not trouble him at all was guilt at breaking the law. He was frightened of being caught and punished, certainly, but he felt no guilt. Then again, perhaps this was precisely *because* of his profession. There had been a time when the law had formed a kind of personality in his mind, and was something he would hate to offend, like a respected schoolteacher or an angry God, but this had long passed. He had seen too many doubtful clients triumph and now regarded the law more as a kind of landscape in which to fight, using its thickets and hollows to catch out one's opponent. Who was right or wrong was merely one aspect of the struggle. What mattered was winning.

So, feeling a slight sweat break out on his neck, he switched off the cellphone and dropped it into the holdall, which he hid behind an old storage heater. The rest of the evening passed surprisingly quietly. The children were away – Ginny at university, Theo at his school – and Peter and his wife ate leftover chicken and watched a documentary about the First World War. Staring at the blurred footage of trenches, Peter slipped between forgetting about the holdall and abruptly remembering it again, and though it scared him, of course, it also filled him with a strange excitement. The next morning he was impatient to revisit his discovery and, telling Harriet that he needed to check the Mini's tax disc, he returned to the garage, where he crouched for some moments, squeezing the packets between his fingers, wondering what it was. Some substances were more valuable than others and he was curious to know how much this was worth. At a whim he reached back into the bag and, his hand trembling slightly, he slipped the cellphone into his jacket pocket.

It was a quiet day at work with just a couple of meetings and he spent most of his time researching a case of disputed planning permission for a car park. As he went through the facts he could sense the cellphone in his pocket, transmitting possibilities. After an hour he surprised himself by suddenly taking it out and pressing the power button. Nothing happened. He returned to his work and had quite forgotten the thing when he was startled by the faint bleeping of 'Speed Bonny Boat'.

'Larry?' This time it was a different voice, one that sounded well educated.

Peter hung up.

All that day he toyed with the idea of switching it on again, and several times he took the phone from his pocket and studied it for a moment or two. The next morning, finally, he pressed the power button. To his surprise it rang almost at once.

'Hi, Larry.'

Again it was a different voice. 'Actually, it's not Larry,' Peter began.

The line went dead.

Peter had had little clear idea of what he would have said and yet he felt strangely annoyed that the caller had rung off. This time he did not switch off the phone. A call came half an hour later.

'Larry?'

Why not at least see what he wanted? 'Larry's gone.'

'Who are you?' The voice sounded wary.

Peter couldn't very well give his real name. He tried to think. 'Jeremy.' It was the name, he realized, of one of his firm's rising young stars.

The caller paused. 'All right then, Jeremy, can you come over? It's sort of urgent.'

Peter scribbled down the address on a piece of Blakeys headed paper.

'So when will you be round?'

Until now Peter felt safe in the fact that he had agreed to nothing. Now he hesitated. If anything decided him it was probably the address, which was in Chelsea: the sort of area he would have liked to live. Why not, he wondered, a little breathless? Just this once? All his life he had lived correctly and where had it got him? He was, he realized, bored with his existence, even with himself, and the thought of doing this warmed him, making him feel like somebody in a film. Besides, he couldn't believe it would be particularly dangerous. Never in all his life had he been stopped by the police: he was not the sort of person they stopped. 'All right,' he agreed. 'I'll come over this evening. Around seven.'

'I need quite a lot,' explained the voice. 'Forty Gs.'

The phrasing baffled Peter for a moment. 'Forty grams?' Peter had never been much good at the metric system.

Suspicion returned to the caller's voice. 'This had better be OK.'

'It will. Don't worry.'

Peter left work early that afternoon and took the tube and bus back to his house, going directly into the garage. How much was forty grams? The packets looked so small and after a moment's indecision he slipped ten of them into his jacket pocket to be sure. That was when he heard the thump of the front door and the faint thud of footsteps from the house: Harriet was home early from her charity, which was bad luck as Peter had been intending to use her kitchen scales to measure out the quantity. So he closed the garage door quietly like a thief and walked to the High Street. The only scales he could find were in a trendy boutique – an Italian device in orange plastic with goofy eyes and splayed feet, that looked better suited to weighing parmesan cheese – and he discreetly weighed one of the bags as he sat on a bench overlooking the river, finding it was exactly ten grams. He was nervous about the exchange, but in the event this proved surprisingly easy. He took the tube to the address and rang the bell of a neat mews house, whose owner – young in his designer jeans and T-shirt – eyed Peter warily as he let him inside. 'So what happened to Larry?'

What indeed? Peter's thoughts turned briefly to the retreating figure of the man who had barged his arm. All he could remember about him was sneakers, a hint of paunch and unwashed black hair. Peter assumed he was safely in jail. 'He went off to the States.'

Another frown. 'He never said anything about that.'

Peter cut short the discussion by handing over the four packets. He had been worrying about what price to charge but fortunately this question solved itself.

'Usual rate?'

Peter nodded and accepted an envelope. Walking back to the tube station his curiosity got the better of him and he stopped at a telephone kiosk. Conveniently shielded by a screen of cards advertising prostitutes, he opened the envelope and, to his own amazement, counted out forty scarlet fifty-pound notes. He grinned all the way home. Two thousand pounds, and not a penny tax to pay. First thing tomorrow he would book the Volvo to be repaired.

By the next evening he had changed his mind about doing just one delivery and he sold twenty grams to a woman in Battersea. Noticing the inflamed area between her nostrils he concluded that the packets contained cocaine. So much the better, as he had never liked the idea of heroin, which seemed a druggy's drug: cocaine was so much classier. The next day, Friday, he bought a new charger cable for the cellphone as its battery was low, and that evening he made two more deliveries. One was to a youthfully grey-haired man in Putney who looked vaguely familiar, so Peter guessed he had seen him on television. The second was to a young couple in Roehampton who gave him a cup of tea.

'I'm glad you've taken over,' the girl told him. 'We never really liked Larry. And sometimes it was days before he'd bother to come over.'

Sitting on the bus home Peter basked in amazement. In three evenings he had accumulated over four thousand five hundred pounds. He had always assumed this world would be full of low-life types, perhaps even deranged by the drugs they were taking, but so far his customers had been from much the same middling to wealthy London milieu as himself. He did not even feel as if he were doing anything very wrong. These were grown-up, educated people, who should know their own minds, and he was giving them what they wanted. Where was the harm in that? He was even quite enjoying the sense of danger and, walking back along Wilmshurst Avenue, he felt more alive than he had in years.

That same evening disaster struck. He and Harriet were sitting watching a programme about Australian animal life when she broke into a frown. 'What's that noise?'

Just audible above the yelps of the sea lions was the faint yet unmistakable sound of 'Speed Bonny Boat'. He had forgotten to switch off the cellphone. 'That's mine,' said Peter, as casually as he was able, and he reached for his jacket. Pressing the receive key he heard the voice of his first customer, the man from Chelsea.

'Jeremy? I know it's rather late, but . . .'

Harriet was looking at him strangely. 'That's not your phone.'

Peter found himself caught awkwardly

between two conversations. 'I'm rather busy just now,' he said into the cellphone. 'Could you ring back tomorrow?'

'But tomorrow's no good. I've got some people coming over here tonight, and . . .'

Peter tried to think of words that would give nothing away. 'I'm sorry,' he said briefly, 'but it's just not possible. Now, look, I really have to go.' He disconnected.

Harriet was staring at him. 'What's going on, Peter?'

'It's just something to do with a case.'

The trouble was that Harriet knew him far too well. 'You're lying. You're so bad at it.' Her voice went quiet. 'Peter, are you having some kind of affair?'

Her accusation took him by surprise, and he felt somehow resentful that she could even imagine such a thing. Now he saw she was struggling not to cry, which he found shocking as Harriet never cried. His mind searched for some harmless explanation for the strange telephone but could find none. How on earth had he got himself into this?

'So you are,' she concluded, her expression crumbling.

'No, no, you don't understand,' he insisted. Anything, even the truth, seemed better than if she believed he was betraying her, as that, he knew, would be the end of them, and he scrabbled for words. 'I . . . found the phone on the common.'

She frowned, unsure. 'What d'you mean?'

It had all gone wrong, as wrong as it could, and he saw no way out now but to finish. 'There was something else I found, too,' he said hopelessly. He could not bring himself to explain, as words seemed to make it all worse. 'I'd better show you.' So he led her into the garage.

For a moment she stood staring at the holdall full of bags, pale with anger. 'You mean you've been . . .' She shook her head in disbelief. 'I simply cannot believe you've done something so stupid.'

He could not believe it himself. How on earth had this seemed a good idea? 'Nobody saw me, I'm sure of it,' he said feebly. 'I'll get rid of all of it tomorrow. I'll throw it in the river. I'll even get rid of the money.' In a rush to show his contrition he took the banknotes from where he had hidden them behind a rusting can of weedkiller.

She looked at the money with new disgust. 'For goodness' sake, how much is there?'

'About four and a half thousand. I'll get rid of it all.'

'What have you been doing, Peter? Did you sell another one like that?' She pointed scornfully at the holdall.

'Oh no.' He picked out ten of the small packets. 'More like that.'

The garage fell into silence. Peter waited for her judgement, praying for some hint that she might, at least one day, be able to forgive him, yet Harriet was not a very forgiving person. They had been together for so long that he could not imagine life alone. The awful possibility occurred to him that she might even report him to the police. It did not seem very likely, and yet she could be so severe. All the while another part of him was hoping against hope that she might somehow let them keep the four thousand five hundred pounds. He had already booked the car to be repaired and wanted to have the window frames painted as they were flaking.

It was only after several long moments passed that he realized, from the hard look on her face, she was not passing judgement after all, but was trying to calculate the total value of the bag.

From that moment onwards Harriet took charge of all arrangements. The next day was a Saturday and she went out after breakfast, returning with a neat electronic weighing machine. 'It says it's accurate to one gram. That should be enough.' Next she moved the bag and the money to the cellar. 'There's no room in that garage.' Finally, impressing Peter with her thoroughness, she counted all of the small packages and checked their weight. 'Some of these aren't correct at all,' she announced disapprovingly. 'I'm surprised you haven't had complaints.'

Peter felt greatly relieved. Aside from the unpleasantness of lying to her, everything was so much easier now: he had a helper and they could even use the car. They made their first delivery that same afternoon, to the customer in Chelsea, taking the Mini as it was better for parking. Harriet stayed in the driving seat – 'We don't want to get clamped' – and three minutes later Peter walked back from the Mews house and handed her the envelope. She counted out the money beneath the dashboard.

'Let's get a Range Rover.'

After that they drove to Kew where Peter delivered twenty grams to a drawn-faced man in an undecorated flat, who hardly said a word during the transaction.

'I don't know much about any of this,' said

Harriet as they drove away, 'but aren't these people buying rather a lot?'

Peter had been wondering, too. 'I think some of them must be selling it on. We're supplying other suppliers.'

'That's a piece of luck. Otherwise it would take for ever.'

From there they went on to a smart house in Richmond, where the customer insisted on making the exchange through the half-closed front door. All that Peter saw of him was a glimpse of grey hair and hooded eyes. Harriet was quite affronted. 'He didn't even let you in.'

'And he only took five grams.'

'Write down his number from the phone. I don't think we should bother with that one again.'

On the way back Harriet parked by a clothing shop on the High Street. 'Don't you think it's time you had a new jacket?'

A few moments later he had one. It was younger in style than what he would normally buy, yet today he somehow did feel younger. He wore it that evening when they went to Corrado's, where they had only been once before, for Ginny's eighteenth, when Peter had struggled hard not to show his anguish at the bill. This time he had no such worries: they ordered a particularly expensive wine and paid in cash. They were just about to go when one of their neighbours walked by. 'I didn't know you came here.'

'From time to time,' said Peter, feeling oddly relaxed.

The neighbour smiled and was about to move on when he turned. 'By the way, I've been meaning to say, we're having a little drinks party on Friday. Do come.'

That night Peter and Harriet made love in a way they had not for years, with a kind of hunger, even a kind of wickedness. Perhaps it was the sense of danger, or of something illicit shared, but Peter could not remember feeling closer to her. The next day they went to the showroom and ordered a Range Rover. Harriet decided it was best to go with the purchase plan and pay from their bank account. 'Otherwise it'll be too obvious. We'll pay for everyday things with the cash.'

The trouble was that cash was flowing in so fast that everyday costs could not begin to keep up. By the end of the next week, despite extensive spending, they had more than nine thousand pounds hidden in the wine box in the cellar. Harriet, who had more free time than Peter, did her best to think of purchases, and soon they had a new fridge, a new television, a new cherry tree in the garden and a new computer. She looked into having an extension built.

'Are you sure we should be getting so many things all at once?' Peter worried. 'The neighbours will notice.'

'They'll just think we've come into some inheritance.'

She was right. Their neighbours in Wilmshurst Avenue seemed to regard the Pelhams' rise to prosperity as being quite in the order of things, even viewing it with relief, as it meant the street was not sullied by a scraped Volvo or flaking window paint. In fact Peter and Harriet found themselves more popular than they had been for a long time. Perhaps because of their new wealth, or simply because they seemed more cheerful these days, the invitation they were extended at Corrado's led to others, until they began to feel almost like new arrivals, and had to turn down invitations as they got in the way of deliveries. At work, too, Peter noticed a change, and he found he was regarded with glances of greater respect by his superiors. He could only guess that this was a consequence of the utter disdain with which he now regarded Blakeys. How could he take it seriously when he earned ten or twenty times as much in a few evening hours as during his long, dreary office day?

'Been somewhere nice, Peter?'

'Actually, no, I haven't been away.'

'Really? Somehow you look like you've been on holiday.'

Not that he would make equity partner – it was far too late for that – but he did find himself given a high-profile case to research. A year before he would have been a little pleased; now he didn't care.

May and June slipped by. Work progressed on the extension, the holdall grew gradually emptier and their list of clients grew, including several new ones who came through word of mouth. Peter found this rather satisfying as he felt it attested to his own reliability. Between their work and their deliveries he and Harriet had never been so busy, and they had to resort to takeaway food and a dog walker for Romulus. And yet for all their long hours they had not felt so well in years. Peter loved the charged feeling in his blood when they drove out in the Mini each evening, and often they would celebrate their sales with love-making. Once, laughing at the very idea, they did it in the hallway on a bed of creased banknotes.

There were awkward moments, too, of course. Peter hated it when a customer called them round and didn't have the money to pay. He firmly refused to give credit and once or twice things got nasty. On several occasions their anonymity was threatened: Peter had to cancel several deliveries when he realized a new client's address was nearby his own house, and once he was forced to hang up in mid-conversation when he recognized a caller as an old acquaintance from university. Probably the worst moment, though, was at a dinner party he and Harriet went to, where conversation was monopolized by a woman recounting the grim details of her daughter's addiction, and her own struggles to have her attend a rehab clinic. The Pelhams sat quietly as the other dinner guests cooed their concern. When they left, Peter found himself feeling decidedly uneasy.

'That was rather dreadful,' he remarked as they walked home.

He had underestimated Harriet's single-mindedness. 'It certainly was. I'm amazed nobody changed the subject. I mean really.'

'I meant it was a terrible story.'

Harriet shrugged. 'The girl should just have known when to stop. It's no different from drinkers and alcoholics.'

Peter frowned. 'I don't know. And what about that woman in Hammersmith they were talking about who was found in her car?'

'What about her? If someone swallows a bottle of aspirins you don't go blaming the chemist.'

'But what if Ginny got mixed up in something like that? Or Theo?'

'Don't be ridiculous. They're both far too sensible.'

Ginny and Theo were much in their thoughts as they would soon be back for the summer holidays. The prospect of their return put Peter and Harriet in a dilemma. Until then the children had only returned for the occasional weekend, which had been easily managed, but two months would be a different matter.

'Perhaps we should just tell the customers that we won't be making any more deliveries till September,' suggested Peter.

'I don't think we can,' considered Harriet. 'They'll go elsewhere and it'll be hard to get them back. Besides, I don't think this is such a problem. Ginny and even Theo will be out a good deal in the evenings and we'll just tell them that we're busy ourselves these days. We can get one of those travelling boxes that you can lock for the cellar, just in case one of them goes down there.'

Matters grew more complicated when Harriet's father, Joe, rang up to say he, too, was coming to stay. This was not a request but an announcement as Joe had helped them buy the house – helped them a good deal – and so had clearly defined visiting rights: the spare room was referred to as 'grandfather's room'. A retired country doctor, he came several times a year to catch up on old friends, to buy things he could not find in local shops and to complain about London. Even now Harriet was not unduly troubled.

'He'll only be here a few days and he goes to bed very early. It'll be fine.'

Peter wondered if they had made the right decision when Ginny – the first to arrive – bombarded them with questions. 'How come you've got all this new stuff?'

The briefest explanation seemed the best. 'We just thought it was time to sort out the house. It's been getting into quite a state.'

'But you always say we can't afford anything.'

'Perhaps we've been overcautious.'

Theo was less questioning. 'Cool computer. Does it burn DVDs?'

Harriet's father was the one least impressed by their purchases. 'I see you've got one of those dreadful cars. Awful tosh. Nobody in the country would touch one.' But he went to bed early, just as Harriet had said, and for several days everything worked out surprisingly well. Ginny went to her summer job at the flower shop during the day and was out on most evenings, while even Theo was fairly busy. Joe was the only one who showed much curiosity about Harriet and Peter's busy evenings. 'Regular gad-abouts these days, aren't you?' he observed disapprovingly. 'Watch out for your livers, that's all I can say.'

One of their nights out was genuine: a neighbour's marquee dinner, which Harriet was determined not to miss. They enjoyed the occasion though there was a price to pay afterwards and the next night saw them hurrying back and forth across London in the Mini to catch up with orders. The traffic was bad and they were late by the time they finally parked near the last address, in Baron's Court. The customer, who looked barely out of his teens, had a smugness that seemed faintly sinister, and he would have been struck off their list except that he bought so freely. Harriet joined Peter for the sale, offering a little comfort in numbers, though on this occasion Peter saw he need not have worried: turning a corner of the long corridor that sounded faintly of pipes, he saw the customer's door was slightly ajar and music was booming out.

'It looks like he's having a party.'

The customer ushered them back into the hallway of the flat, where it was quieter. 'Cool. I was getting worried you weren't going to make it.'

'Twenty grams?' checked Peter. Harriet, efficient as ever, had already measured out the amount and in a moment the packets and the money had been exchanged. Peter and Harriet were just turning to leave when something made them stop: a peal of laughter that rang out from the closed door beside them. It was, unmistakably, Ginny. Peter felt pulled in two directions. He was appalled, of course, by the thought of his daughter – his baby – being in a place like this. But to intervene . . . 'Come on, let's just leave,' he told Harriet, trying to take her arm.

She pushed him away with an angry look. 'Let go of me.'

The customer was looking puzzled. 'What's up?'

Harriet was already reaching for the door and so, with a dull sense of rising disaster like an itch, Peter followed her into what he saw was the kitchen, its table strewn with packets of crisps. For just a fraction of a second before she saw them, Peter saw Ginny, leaning against a cupboard, her head thrown back and her eyes half closed in delight at whatever had made her laugh. Between her fingers was a long, neatly rolled joint. Then her smile fell away.

'Oh, God.'

Peter peered round the room and it was then that he saw Theo, his mouth hanging open in amazement. This grew worse and worse.

'You're both coming home this moment,' said Harriet tersely.

The children stood up in shocked obedience and for one, brief, moment Peter hoped Harriet might somehow get away with this, but then a defiant look came into Ginny's eyes. 'What the hell are you doing here anyway? Have you been following me?'

Even now it might have been all right except for the customer, who broke into a strange laugh. 'You mean these are your folks, Ginnsy? But they've just sold me twenty Gs of best coke.'

The room fell into a profound silence. The handful of other guests stared and a girl with a navel ring let out a kind of giggle. Theo frowned in new wonderment. Ginny was staring at her parents with the strangest look. 'What's going on?'

Peter felt oddly quiet, the stillness of complete despair. Everything was ruined, without question, and yet even now, when it was far too late, his instinct was to try to keep things quiet. 'Let's go home.'

This time Ginny did not argue and they tramped down the long carpeted corridors in silence and crammed themselves into the Mini. 'Now I understand how you got all that stuff,' said Ginny, sounding almost as if she might cry. 'I just don't believe this.'

Peter tried to think of something to make things look better. There was nothing, nothing at all. 'It was an accident. We found it on the common.'

Harriet, as ever, was more aggressive. 'At least we don't take the stuff.'

Ginny was outraged. 'I had a joint, Mum. I'd never touch coke.'

'Oh?' said Harriet almost primly. 'Then why was he buying it?'

'Toby? Toby would take anything.'

It was then that the interior of the car was filled with the sound of 'Speed Bonny Boat'. Peter, driving, reached into his pocket. 'Yes?'

The voice was unfamiliar. 'Jeremy? I need thirty grams. It's sort of urgent.'

'This really isn't a good time.'

'I can come to you,' the voice offered. 'Give me your address?'

'Wilmshurst Av—' Peter stopped himself. As if things weren't bad enough already now he was telling some stranger where they lived. 'Look I can't help you.' He rang off.

'Another customer?' asked Ginny acidly.

'I don't know how you could take Theo to a place like that,' said Harriet in instant counter-attack.

'He took me,' said Ginny indignantly. 'Toby's his friend, not mine.'

Yet another blow. Theo had always been the good one, or so they thought. Peter drove slowly through suburban streets, not wanting to arrive.

'Is that true?' Harriet demanded.

Theo was undaunted, alarmingly so. 'I want

a new computer,' he replied casually. 'A really good laptop.'

'What?'

'The thing I've got is ancient. Nobody at school has them any more. And you got all that stuff for yourselves.'

'You haven't answered my question.'

They had reached Wilmshurst Avenue and Peter was just opening the car door when he again heard 'Speed Bonny Boat'.

'Yes?' he snapped.

'I rang just now.'

'I told you,' said Peter angrily. 'I just can't—' Puzzlingly the line went dead, but even then Peter did not make the connection. Nor did he when, from the corner of his eye, he noticed a car creeping slowly towards them along the street. But he did, finally, when it drew to a halt just in front of theirs and three men clambered out, two bulging in their shirts. They looked so much like something out of a cheap film that for an instant, despite his rising fear, Peter almost wanted to laugh.

'I guessed you'd be somewhere round here,' said the smaller of the three, 'as that's where Larry got took.'

'Who's this?' asked Ginny. Even Harriet looked uneasy. The family crisis was forgotten, at least for now.

'I don't know,' said Peter, though he could guess. Oddly enough this possibility – that someone might come to reclaim the holdall – had hardly occurred to him until then, he had thought of it so much as something owed to him.

'Roy,' the stranger introduced himself. 'Shall we have our chat inside?'

Once they were off the street they would be helpless in the face of . . . Of what? Peter wondered if he should kick up a fuss and try to attract attention from the other houses – their lights were on – in the hope that Roy might panic and leave them be. But he knew deep down that this was beyond him: even now he could not bear the thought of the neighbours witnessing their shame. Peter meekly turned the key, aware of a strange sense of unreality as he held open the door for Roy and his two helpers, with their faint odour of sweating muscle and their swollen shoulders that brushed against the door frame.

'You don't look the part,' observed Roy. 'You look like you should be working in a bank. Nice house.' Even in his compliments there was an audible menace.

Peter tried to appear equal to the situation, hardening his voice. 'What d'you want?'

It was an unwise move, provoking Roy to show his power, and he grabbed Peter by the collar, then pushed him away so that he almost lost his balance. 'What d'you think I want, Four Eyes? A ticket to the ballet? Larry only paid the up-front. You owe me twenty-five K.'

Peter had never been brave and he would comply with any demand – comply eagerly – if it meant there would be no trouble. For a moment he panicked himself with thoughts of injuries to faces, eyes, fingers. Twenty-five thousand? What if they did not have enough? For the last few weeks he and Harriet had been too busy to count up their takings, so he had no idea how much they had. Already he regretted spending so much on the new television, the fridge and that damn cherry tree.

Harriet, to his shock, was on another tack entirely. 'But that's our money. We earned it.'

'Harriet, please.' Peter tried to quiet her, amazed by her lack of instinct.

'You didn't earn it,' Roy corrected her. 'You nicked it.'

'We're the ones who've been driving all round London making deliveries.'

'So?'

The last thing that would have occurred to Peter at this moment was that something else could go wrong, but it did. A voice called out from the top of the stairs. 'What on earth's going on?' Harriet's father was staring down at them, looking like a set of bones in pyjamas.

'Dad's been selling coke,' said Ginny simply.

He looked puzzled. 'That awful brown drink?'

'Cocaine.'

The old man's mouth opened in wonder and he stared at Peter with a mixture of disgust and glee. 'A druggy! My daughter's married to a druggy. I always knew there was something funny about you.'

Peter hardly cared. What difference could this make? He might as well put up a sign by the door, Peter Pelham, Cocaine Vendor.

Roy, though, was losing patience. 'I don't want to spoil the party but can you give me my fucking money?'

'Who's that?' demanded Joe.

'I'm the debt collector, grandpa. And if I don't get paid nice and quick I'll start getting very annoyed.'

The hall fell silent as even Joe sensed danger.

'It's here,' said Peter, leading the way to the cellar. For some reason – a kind of redundant squeamishness – he disliked the idea of Ginny, Theo and Harriet's father seeing what was down there, but he could hardly stop them, and soon the cellar was crowded with people, all watching as he opened the travelling box and removed the holdall of bags – still a good third full – and took out the Fortnum's hamper basket beneath, full of banknotes that Harriet had sorted neatly into different denominations. Peter rather assumed Roy would take it all, but no.

'Go on, start counting.'

It took so long. Every now and then Peter would glance round and see them all silently staring: Ginny, Theo, Harriet, her father, Roy and his two muscled helpers. Was money that interesting? It seemed it was. As the minutes passed, and his mumbled numbers climbed from five to ten and on into the teens and twenties, with still lots to go, Peter began to relax. There would be enough. More than enough, in fact: as he counted out the last note there was still a large heap remaining.

Roy scooped the money into a plastic bag. 'I'll say goodnight then.' He gave a faint laugh. 'Just don't do it again.'

They all marched back up the stairs and Peter found himself seeing Roy and his two thugs to the door like so many dinner guests. Roy was about to step out into the street when he stopped. 'Tell me, how long did it take you to make that stash?'

Peter eyed him suspiciously. What was he after now? 'A couple of months.'

'That's not bad, you know. Better than Larry, any day, lazy little slug.' He thought for a moment. 'When you're finished with that lot would you like another?'

Peter gave a kind of half-laugh. 'Definitely not.'

Saturday morning broke quietly over the Pelham household. Peter woke with a shock, having dreamed that none of this had happened and, opening his eyes, he saw Harriet already dressed. 'I'm going down,' she told him, her face set. 'I'm damned if I'm going to let her lecture me.'

As Peter washed and shaved he found himself wondering if he should pack a bag. Did the police let you take one, or was he thinking of Nazis in wartime films? Creeping downstairs, like an intruder in his house, he could hear Harriet and Ginny's voices from the sitting room. Rather to his surprise, Ginny sounded frustrated, like a tennis player searching vainly for a smash shot. 'What d'you mean, understand? You're the ones who were always going on about the evils of drugs.'

Peter shuffled towards the kitchen, concentrating on the simple and comforting thought of breakfast, though he left the door ajar to hear. Harriet's voice was slow and calm so he missed half her words, but he caught 'lives haven't been easy', 'your poor father', 'money worries' and 'your and Theo's education'. She finished with a triumphantly audible, 'I'm not saying everything we did was right but we did it for you.' Peter found himself impressed: she was almost making it seem like this was Ginny's fault, and it occurred to him that Harriet would make a damn good barrister. Far better than Ginny, whose voice was shrill and excitable as she lost the battle for self-control.

'You're making yourself sound like Mother Theresa. You're a pair of drug pushers, for God's sake.'

'Don't be absurd, Ginny, we never pushed anything. People rang us. It was all we could do to keep up.' Harriet's voice was almost prim. 'And we never touched it ourselves.'

'Most people would say you should be in jail.'

Peter shuddered slightly over the coffee machine.

'Sometimes,' said Harriet serenely, 'you have to take risks for the good of your family.'

Ginny's voice rang out as she opened the door to the hall. 'This is just obscene. It's like I don't know who you are,' and with that she clumped up the stairs. He who holds the battlefield wins the victory, Peter thought to himself, but then the distressing realization came to him that he and Harriet had just thrown away any remaining influence they had over their daughter: never again would they be able to tell her off for being late or drunk or having the wrong boyfriend. The idea would have been more disturbing except that there were others who were far worse, such as the half-dozen party guests who had been in Toby's kitchen. They were sure to recount what they had seen – it was not every day that you found your friends' mum and dad selling cocaine – and the story would travel. Not for the first time Peter spooked himself into thinking he heard a sudden knock at the door, but it was Joe, plodding down the stairs. This would be more trouble. Or would it? Peter was surprised to see he was carrying his suitcase.

'Harriet,' he called out, sounding almost subdued. 'I want you to take me to the station. I'm going home.'

Peter assumed the crisis would rise to some final, terrible climax but instead the rest of the day was quiet, as Ginny strode about the house in angry silence. Worse was to come. A couple of days after Toby's party – or 'that night' as Peter and Harriet now referred to it – she appeared in the sitting room as they were watching the news. 'Jean's asked me to go with her to church this Sunday, so I'll be out all morning.'

Jean worked with her at the flower shop, but before now Ginny had talked of her disparagingly, describing her as 'a real little God Squad', so there was no mistaking the significance of this announcement. Ginny – rebel Ginny, with her Green views and her radical chic clothes – going to church? The idea appalled Peter. 'Right you are,' he answered lamely.

Theo struck the next day. Curiously enough Peter had not been so worried about him, as he had seemed relatively unaffected, and his only protest had been to avoid family meals, which Peter suspected sprang more from convenience than principle, allowing him to play computer games in his room without interruption. Then Peter came home from work one evening and found his son slumped on the sofa smoking a cigarette.

'That's a very dirty habit,' was all that Peter could think of saying.

'Is it, Dad?' Theo answered with a smirk.

The next day Peter found him smoking a long, neatly rolled joint. 'Theo . . .' Peter began.

Theo feigned wide-eyed curiosity. 'Yes, Dad?'

'Can't you at least do that outside?' Peter left the room rather than witness his demand being ignored. The thought returned to him as he tramped purposelessly up the stairs, 'He who holds the battlefield . . .'

It was that night that Peter finally decided to

dispose of the holdall of bags. They had given some thought as to methods (in the rubbish? But what if it burst in the dustcart and someone noticed?) and had decided to fling it into the river. Harriet had spent hours in their bathroom carefully wiping clean all the packets with paper towels and washing-up liquid to remove any fingerprints. Was all of this his and Harriet's punishment, Peter wondered as he drove the Mini through the quiet suburban streets? No, even if matters calmed down he knew that nothing would ever be the same. Irreligious though he was, some part of him accepted the idea of universal retribution. And yet it was so unfair. Other people got away with all kinds of things. What about their neighbours with their million-pound annual bonuses and golden handshakes and share options: were they all so clean? Why couldn't he, Peter Pelham, win, just for once?

He parked close to the point where the tow-path left the road and vanished behind trees. The moment could hardly have been better: a faint drizzle was falling, keeping people indoors, and the river was at high tide, ready to carry the bag away. Yet Peter did not hurry to take the holdall from the boot, but remained in his seat. Something was changing in his thoughts, and his anger was shifting target, like a gun on its platform. He hated the holdall of bags, certainly, but even more he was furious at how much it had cost them. What had they got out of all of this? Ten thousand? – he didn't even know the exact amount – plus an extension to the house and a few other trinkets. And for this they had thrown their lives into turmoil and lost the respect of their children. What made Peter angriest of all, though, was the thought that they had had to pay off Roy for what Peter still thought of as his windfall. For that matter, they had paid that lowlife for all these remaining packets that he was now about to throw into the river. It was a thought that was hard to get past: that he would be hurling away something that he had bought, and at such a painful cost. It seemed so wasteful.

Peter stared at the windscreen, speckled with tiny dots of rain, and allowed his task of the evening to shimmer with uncertainty. What was the rush, he asked himself, already warming to the new line. Several days had passed and there had been no police knocking at the door. He no longer felt so worried by Toby's party guests, guessing they were unlikely to tell drug anecdotes except to other druggies. A seagull flew above the river, lit by the street lights. Peter watched as the rain on the windscreen merged into a blur, then he turned the ignition key and, the holdall of bags still in the boot, drove home.

Opening the front door he walked straight through the house and, taking a torch, he followed the circle of light to the greenhouse. The largest space was beside a sapling mulberry tree, and this was where he carefully buried the holdall with its packets and cellphone, scattering the excess soil on other flowerbeds. It was only when he had finished and began walking back towards the house that he saw Harriet's silhouette in the bathroom window, watching him. For a moment he froze. Would she be furious? But when he walked into the bedroom he saw no accusation in her eyes.

'Will it be safe there, d'you think?' was all she asked.

Neither of them made any mention of the bag during the remainder of the summer. As the weeks passed, the children went from bad to worse. Theo began to come home drunk and seemed to take pleasure in leaving the dog-ends of joints about the house: once Peter even found one stubbed out in the butter dish. On several occasions he or Harriet were goaded into protest, but to no effect, as Theo simply smirked, 'That's good, coming from you.'

Ginny's evolution was marked by sudden appearances in the sitting room that seemed increasingly like ambushes. 'Jean and I have decided to join Simon's discussion group,' she announced one Sunday, wearing the frumpy clothes that she now preferred to radical chic.

Simon, needless to say, was the priest. 'Simon's so amazing, he makes the world seem a cleaner place,' she told them a few days later with a disapproving glance. 'Really, you should come. He said he'd like to see you.' Peter wondered glumly what she had told him. A week later, with a look of solemn concern, she declared, 'Jean and I prayed for you this afternoon.'

Harriet could barely contain her fury. 'She's doing it deliberately.' But even then she could see nothing – nothing at all – that they could do. It came as a great relief when September arrived and the children finally left for their autumn terms. It was Harriet who first raised the question of the bag of bags. 'What now?'

Peter had given the matter thought. 'We could try and sell it back to Roy, I suppose. His number should still be on the cellphone. And we've paid for it, after all.' He had thought the suggestion quite radical but once again he had underestimated Harriet.

'He'll hardly give us a penny, and I'm damned

if I'm going to chuck it away for nothing after all we've been through.'

'Then . . .?' Peter found himself uneasy at the idea of resuming their deliveries, but he said nothing. It was ludicrous, but he felt a kind of playground reluctance to be seen as scared, especially by his wife. 'Are you sure that's a good idea?'

'It didn't seem very dangerous before,' Harriet insisted briskly. 'And it would get rid of it.'

That same night, walking briskly to disguise the sick feeling in his stomach, Peter went with her to the greenhouse and they dug up the holdall. After almost two months of disconnection it was not enough simply to recharge the cellphone; they had to renew contact themselves. Fortunately Harriet – efficient as ever – had listed customers' numbers and addresses in a ruled notebook. Peter made the calls and found himself coolly received.

'I know exactly who you are. So you've

finally decided to switch on your phone, have you?'

It did not take them very long to return to their routine of the spring. And yet nothing was quite the same. Rather than diminishing, Peter's uneasiness grew stronger, and he found himself increasingly plagued by panic. As he walked to a customer's door he imagined a gang of police waiting just inside, while the sight of a police car – even speeding away in the opposite direction – was enough to make him break into a sweat, he began to have difficulty sleeping, and he became insistent on taking precautions, such as parking several streets away from a customer's door.

'What difference does it make?' complained Harriet. 'You still have to go there. It just makes everything take longer.'

'They might be taking down number plates.'

Rather to his own surprise he found himself struck with attacks of conscience, which came upon him quite unexpectedly, when he was sitting at his desk at work, or brushing his teeth.

Strangely enough, the face that troubled him at these times was never Ginny's, as he would have expected, but was that of her church friend Jean, whom he had only met once very briefly at the door: a dumpy-looking girl with self-assured eyes. He could picture her precisely, shaking her large, round face in stolid disapproval. The only answer he could find for her stare was, rather lamely, that this would soon all be over: the holdall was steadily emptying. As weeks passed Peter became increasingly anxious to speed up the process, taking on almost any order, regardless of how late and tired this made Harriet and himself.

'The Cotswolds are just criminal these days,' Harriet complained one rainy night when only a couple of dozen packets remained. 'Thirty-five thousand won't get us a mortgage on a pigpen.' She had sole charge of planning how they might spend their money – Peter found he was curiously indifferent – and had rung various country estate agents.

'Then perhaps we shouldn't get a house after all,' said Peter warily, sensing what was coming. 'We can always go off on weekend breaks to hotels.'

Harriet lost her temper. 'But I thought we were agreed that a place in the country is what this is all for. Besides, almost everybody else has had one for years.' There was no missing the accusation in her voice, one that Peter had often heard in the days before the black holdall of packets, suggesting that he had let her down, robbing her of the life she had expected. 'We can't stop now.'

'For goodness sake, Harriet,' he complained. 'We haven't even worked out how to get this money into our bank account and now you're saying we should get another bag.'

'Have we had one bad moment since we started this? No, not one.'

Peter said nothing, hating himself for his silence. But it was hard: she was so interminably fearless. Besides, she was right, they had had absolutely no trouble with their deliveries. And so, that same windy October night, they went to the greenhouse and dug up several bin liners of cash, then drove out to meet Roy and purchased their second bag of bags. Peter felt strangely numb as he drove back, listening to Harriet's complaints.

'He's just a lazy middleman. We pay him almost half our takings and he doesn't do a damn thing. He doesn't go anywhere or take any risks. If we could only go to the suppliers.'

Peter shot her a disbelieving look. 'What? In Colombia or Bolivia or wherever it is?'

'Why not? That's where they grow this stuff, the cocoa plants, or whatever they're called. We should deal directly with them.'

This time, though, even Harriet realized she had overreached herself and she did not raise the subject again. Instead she became increasingly focused on their business efficiency. She bought an accounts book, just as if they were running a tobacconist's shop or a sandwich bar, and at the end of each week she carefully wrote down their takings before depositing them in the greenhouse in a fresh black bin bag, just as others would deposit their takings in the bank. As for Peter, the renewed supply of endless small packages seemed to fill him with an even greater sense of urgency, and on some evenings they did as many as eight or nine deliveries, returning at one in the morning. These days there were no thoughts of love-making on creased banknotes, as they were far too tired, and they went up to bed without a word.

It was in mid-November that Harriet's father rang. 'I'm coming down for a few days.'

It was bad news. As well as the inconvenience – they would have to cut down on their deliveries – Peter anticipated no end of scornful moralizing. But as they all sat in the kitchen with tea and biscuits, he was surprised to see how quiet Joe seemed. 'I've rung quite a few times in the evening,' he said at last, 'but you always seem to be out.'

Harriet shot him a warning look. 'What if we are?'

A strange, insistent look came into Joe's eyes. 'I could be very useful, you know.'

Only now did Peter finally understand. If he hadn't felt so sick about everything he might have laughed. He felt, if anything, a kind of satisfaction that Joe was, after all, no better than he himself. A few months was all it had taken for the remembrance of those crisp red and purple banknotes to ferment in his mind. Sure enough, Joe began listing his needs, in a curiously whining voice, as if he had been unfairly deprived. 'And the house hasn't been decorated since before Julia died. I really can't live like that. For that matter, I need a new car, too. Something bigger, for the dogs.'

Peter and Harriet discussed his offer as they lay in bed. Harriet was not keen. 'He won't know what he's doing. He'll be a liability.'

Peter, surprisingly, was enthusiastic, drawn by the thought of getting rid of the packets more quickly. 'I think he could be very helpful,' he considered through a yawn. 'You can go out with him during the day when I'm at work. That way we might even get this next bag finished before Christmas.'

First he would have to be trained. It was years since Joe had driven in London, which he might have to do if parking wardens appeared when he was minding the car. They decided he should sit in the back of the Mini for a few evenings. It was on the second of these that everything went wrong. Probably this was bound to occur eventually, as Peter and Harriet's drug dealing had now become a kind of headlong rush, tempting disaster. The end came on a black, rainy night in late November, when they were driving through Ealing in the Mini. It was proving a frustrating evening, as their first customer had had no money to pay, giving them a wasted journey. Now they had seven more deliveries to go and were already late, delayed by the traffic, which was heavy with the approach of Christmas.

'Can't you drive, you ninny?' Peter complained when the car in front stalled and made them miss a green light. When the lights finally came round he revved up the engine in annoyance and sped through the junction. It was not so much that he saw the problem too late as that he never saw it at all, and as he slowed down at the next lights he was aware of a thump against the side of the car.

'Oh, for God's sake,' Harriet groaned. 'It's a bloody cyclist.'

Peter, exasperated by their delays, would probably have driven straight on, but this was impossible as the Mini was already stuck in the next queue of traffic. There was a sharp rap against the window and when Peter wound it down he saw a surprisingly short figure draped in reflective yellow plastic.

'Can't you look where you're going?' The cyclist held up a slither of white plastic. 'And you've done for my back light. That cost me five ninety-nine.'

Afterwards Peter would often think of that face: a foolish-looking face, with small eyes and sticking-out ears: a face that one would never imagine might prove one's nemesis. Although, in truth, it was Peter himself who was the real cause of his own destruction. If only he had slept better during the previous weeks he might have apologized for what was, after all, his own fault. Instead he was overcome by a strange obstinacy. 'You should have been looking.'

'Silly oaf,' agreed Joe.

It was Harriet, normally so oblivious, who saw clearly. 'Why not just give him the money, Peter?'

Peter replied as if she had criticized him. 'It was his fault.'

By now the traffic ahead was beginning to move and, worried they might escape, the cyclist darted round the Mini and stood in front of the bonnet, blocking the way. 'I'm not shifting till I get my five ninety-nine.'

Car horns began to sound behind them and Peter added to the din with his own, then leant out of the window. 'Can you please get out of the way?'

Even Joe was beginning to grow doubtful. 'Perhaps we should just give him the money.'

Harriet was more practical and fiddled in her purse. 'I'm sure I have a ten in here.'

Peter later wondered, not infrequently, what road his life might have followed if he had accepted their advice. Ten pounds? It seemed hard to believe he had refused when they were awash with cash. At the time, though, there had been no room for such logic, as his head was entirely filled with a kind of roaring din of irritation. All he could think of was that he was late, that customers were waiting, that the traffic was as bad as could be, and now this damnable midget with sticking-out ears was stopping him from moving. He turned the door handle and unwisely climbed out of the car. 'Get out of the way.'

The cyclist met his glare. 'Five ninety-nine.'

They were more easily matched than one might have thought. The cyclist was shorter, it was true, but he was young and fit, at least compared to Peter. The difficulty was that neither had any real comprehension of how to fight, and so they stood there, scowling and raising their hands as if they might push at each other.

Harriet had wound down her window. 'Peter, for God's sake, there's a policeman coming.'

Finally Peter realized the danger. Yet fear can work in strange ways. Rather than trying to defuse the situation – with an apology and Harriet's ten-pound note – he instead became more impatient to end the matter and he shoved at his enemy, pushing him clear of the bonnet. His success was short-lived, and as he marched back round the car the cyclist darted after him, clutching his sleeve.

'No you don't, grandpa.'

By the time the policeman reached them they were engaged in an amateurish tussle. Even at this late stage there was still an element of chance: it was inevitable that the policeman would try to prise them apart, but not that his hand would push against – of all places – the front pocket of Peter's blazer. As he pressed Peter back there was a faint popping sound, like a seaweed bubble bursting, and a white cloud appeared momentarily before Peter's eyes. He felt a soft coating on his face and involuntarily licked his lips, tasting a sharp, tangy flavour – it was the only taste of it he would ever know – and for just an instant he felt a strange glow of excited well-being.

The policeman was staring at him with a puzzled look. 'What's that on your nose?'

Peter guessed he was doomed, but he might at least limit the extent of the disaster, and so he made a pretence of losing his balance and fell against the car, murmuring into Harriet's window, 'It was all me. You don't know anything.'

# Powder

Neighbours and old acquaintances of the Pelhams were intrigued, even quietly thrilled, by their sudden fall. Peter and Harriet had seemed so respectable, to the point of dreariness, that there was a kind of perfection about their arrest, which enriched the grey November weather. By summer it was impossible to get away from their story even if one had wanted to, as the trial was covered on television and in the papers every day. Inadvertently the Pelhams had become notorious: Peter's descent from dull propriety to drugs pusher was so sheer that it instantly placed him in that pantheon of characters who float before the nation to be cheered or booed. For months the soft suburban air hummed with talk.

'Actually, I did notice that they were always coming and going late at night, but I assumed they were just very sociable.'

'And they had it all buried in their greenhouse . . .'

There were some who felt pity for Peter Pelham, whether from natural generosity, or from a vague unease that something similar might one day happen to themselves. Others felt he had received nothing less than his just desserts. But was this really true? Yes, jail came as a terrible shock to Peter, and he hated the banging doors, the shared rooms, the simmering brutality, the lingering smell of urine and disinfectant. Finding himself in the same wing as Larry was particularly bad luck. Harriet's visits were strained, while he dreaded those by Ginny, who plagued him with her forgiveness. It was a relief to him that Theo never came.

And yet, as the weeks turned to months, Peter slowly began to adjust to his new life. He found he had protectors, who showed a certain admiration for somebody who had been given every privileged advantage and yet, just like themselves, had been unable to resist risking all. And so it was that Peter sometimes woke in the middle of the night to find himself filled with a glow of unexpected satisfaction. The fact was that he was famous. A newspaper wanted his story. He had received sack loads of letters from complete strangers, and though some were accusing, others were not, and a young woman from Scarborough had even invited him to spend the night with her in a hotel room. People he had never met thought of him as dangerously exciting. So in a way he had achieved what he had hungered for that bright spring evening when he first heard the beeping of 'Speed Bonny Boat'. Peter Pelham was somebody.

**Meanwhile, many thousands of miles away . . .**

# PICADOR SHOTS

SHALOM AUSLANDER
'Holocaust Tips for Kids' and 'Smite the Heathens, Charlie Brown' from *Beware of God*

CRAIG DAVIDSON
'A Mean Utility' and 'Life in the Flesh' from *Rust and Bone*

BRET EASTON ELLIS
'Water from the Sun' and 'Discovering Japan' from *The Informers*

NELL FREUDENBERGER
'Lucky Girls' from *Lucky Girls*

ALEKSANDAR HEMON
'Exchange of Pleasant Words' and 'A Coin' from *The Question of Bruno*

JACKIE KAY
'Sonata' from *Wish I Was Here*

MATTHEW KNEALE
'Powder' from *Small Crimes in An Age of Abundance*

CLAIRE MESSUD
'The Professor's History'

JAMES SALTER
'My Lord You' and 'Palm Court' from *Last Night*

COLM TÓIBÍN
'The Use of Reason' from *Mothers and Sons*

NIALL WILLIAMS
unpublished new story – 'The Unrequited'

TIM WINTON
'Small Mercies' from *The Turning*

All collections are available in Picador.